Let's Go
HUNTING

Suzanne Slade

WITHDRAWN

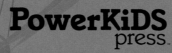

PowerKiDS press.

New York

To Amelie, Rachel, and Joanne—for all your help and encouragement

Published in 2007 by The Rosen Publishing Group, Inc.
29 East 21st Street, New York, NY 10010

First Edition

Editor: Amelie von Zumbusch
Book Design: Dean Galiano and Erica Clendening
Layout Design: Julio Gil

Photo Credits: Cover, pp. 8, 12, 22, 26 © www.shutterstock.com; p. 4 © Dale C. Spartas/Corbis; p. 6 U.S. Fish and Wildlife Service; p. 7 U.S. Fish and Wildlife Service. Photo by Ryan Hagerty; p. 7 U.S. Fish and Wildlife Service. Photo by Richard Enriquez; p. 11 © www.istockphoto.com/John-Mark Romans; pp. 14, 16, 28 © Digital Stock; p. 17 NPS Photo by Stan Canter; pp. 18, 25 © Getty Images; p. 20 © www.istockphoto.com/Kevin Miller; p. 21 © www.istockphoto.com/Jostein Hauge; p. 24 © Digital Vision; p. 28 (inset) © www.istockphoto.com/Deo Abesamis.

Library of Congress Cataloging-in-Publication Data

Slade, Suzanne.
  Let's go hunting / Suzanne Slade. — 1st ed.
    p. cm. — (Adventures outdoors)
  Includes bibliographical references and index.
  ISBN-13: 978-1-4042-3646-2 (library binding)
  ISBN-10: 1-4042-3646-5 (library binding)
  1. Hunting—Juvenile literature. I. Title.
  SK35.5 .S
  799.2—dc22
                                                    2006019561

Manufactured in the United States of America

Contents

The Sport of Hunting

People all over the world like to hunt. Hunting is a great way for kids and adults to explore nature together. Hunters enjoy observing wildlife. They study the habits of animals that live in forests and around lakes. It is exciting and challenging to use what you have learned about animal behavior to help you hunt for animals.

Some people hunt for sport, or fun. These hunters may stuff and display their animals. Other people hunt for food to eat. It makes a hunter feel proud to bring meat home for a tasty family dinner. Some people use animal fur or hides to make clothes, belts, or other useful things. Hunting is a sport that brings you closer to nature.

This young hunter has caught a pair of pheasant. Pheasant are one of the most popular birds for hunting.

Where to Hunt

Proper planning is the key to a successful hunt. Even when you go hunting near your home, you might need reservations to hunt in certain areas. If you want to hunt in another state, you may need to mail forms to that state in advance. Wherever you hunt, remember to look for and obey No Hunting signs.

A hunting preserve is one of the best places to hunt. Preserves are large areas that are reserved for

Hunters need duck stamps to hunt migratory birds. Migratory birds move with the seasons.

These people are hunting at the Horicon National Wildlife Refuge in southeastern Wisconsin.

DID YOU KNOW?

Most states require you to purchase a permit called a hunting license before you go hunting.

hunters. Many kinds of wild **game**, such as deer, **elk**, **pheasant**, ducks, **quail**, and turkeys, live in preserves. If you ask permission, farmers might allow you to hunt on their private land. Sometimes farmers need to reduce the population of certain wild animals on their farmland.

Hunting Clothes

Hunters wear special clothes that keep them dry, comfortable, and safe. They must also choose clothing that allows them to move quickly. Most hunters wear several layers of clothes. The outer layer is for protection from the weather. Layers of clothing may be added under the top layer for warmth.

Long pants help protect hunters from sharp branches and thorns. Many states require hunters to wear a bright orange piece of clothing. This helps hunters recognize each other and prevents accidental shootings. When hunting at close range for animals such as turkeys or ducks, hunters often wear **camouflage** clothing. This green and brown spotted clothing helps hunters hide from animals.

This hunter's orange vest makes it easy for other hunters to see him.

Learning to Hunt

One way to start learning about how to hunt is to read books about the sport. You should also find an adult who can teach you more about hunting gear and safety.

Hunters often go to a shooting range to practice using a gun or bow and arrow. Shooting ranges usually have indoor and outdoor **targets**. Large

This boy is learning how to hold and shoot a gun at a shooting range.

targets are placed at close range for beginning shooters. More advanced shooters can aim at small targets at longer ranges. Hunters can also practice aiming at moving targets called clay pigeons at a shooting range. A clay pigeon is a heavy, round disc. A machine called a trap throws the clay pigeons into the air.

The orange disc in the middle of this picture is a clay pigeon.

12

Guns and Hunting

There are several types of guns you can use when hunting. Different guns work best for hunting different animals. For large game, such as deer or elk, hunters generally use a rifle. A rifle has a long, thin **barrel** and shoots a lead bullet. Hunters look through a sight or **scope** mounted on the rifle to aim at their target.

A shotgun is used for hunting small animals and **waterfowl**. A shell is shot out of the long, fat barrel of a shotgun. The shell holds many tiny, metal balls, called buckshot. When a shotgun is fired, it sprays pieces of buckshot over a large area, making it easier to hit small animals.

You can see the thin barrel on this young man's rifle. *Inset:* This girl is checking her shotgun.

Big and Small Game

Big game hunting and small game hunting are both popular in the United States. Big game animals include deer, elk, moose, black bears, and pronghorn. Hunting for big game can be very challenging. Hunters must sometimes walk several miles (km) over rough ground to find big game animals. If a big game hunter is successful, the heavy animal must also be carried back.

Small game hunting is the most common type of hunting. This sport is a favorite among hunters because small game is generally easy to find. People hunt small game animals, such as rabbit, hare, raccoon, and squirrels, for sport and food. A new hunter might start by trying to bag, or catch, a squirrel or rabbit. These animals are especially plentiful in most areas.

Pronghorn are one of the world's fastest animals. They can run 60 miles per hour (97 km/h)!

A raccoon has a striped tail and a dark stripe, or mask, across its eyes.

Hunters use a skill called scouting to locate animals. When scouting an area, hunters look for animal tracks, **scat**, feeding spots, or bedding areas. These clues help them know what kind of animals are nearby.

When a hunter finds an animal, the hunter must decide whether to stand hunt or stalk hunt. Stand hunters stay in one place and hide while waiting for an animal to walk by. This method works well near a heavily traveled trail or feeding area. Stalk hunting is useful when a hunter sees an animal that is far away. A stalk hunter moves slowly and quietly toward the animal. Hiding along the way, a stalk hunter waits until he or she is at close range to fire.

Hunters use both stand hunting and stalk hunting when they are trying to bag an elk.

Fowling

Hunting for fowl, or birds, is called fowling. Hunters use either guns or traps to go fowling. There are two groups of birds that people hunt. They are upland game birds and waterfowl.

Upland game birds spend most of their time on land. Pheasant, quail, grouse, partridge, and turkeys are all upland birds. These birds have very keen hearing, so a hunter must be very quiet around them. Hunters almost always use shotguns when hunting upland birds.

Birds that spend most of their time in or around water are called waterfowl. Waterfowl can see color better than people can. For this reason hunters hide in **blinds** while hunting waterfowl.

Hunters use decoys, or fake ducks, to draw live ducks to them. Decoys are made from wood, foam, or plastic.

Hunting with Dogs

A well-trained dog can be a hunter's best friend. Several breeds, such as Cocker spaniels, English pointers, and beagles, are often used as hunting dogs. Besides keeping a hunter company on a long trip, hunting dogs have special skills. A dog that is good at flushing, pointing, or retrieving is very useful.

A flushing dog will creep through thick ground cover and scare birds out so the hunter can see

Labrador retrievers were bred to be hunting dogs. Today they are also popular as pets.

Gordon setters are hunting dogs that were bred to hunt birds, such as pheasant and quail.

them. Pointing dogs have a keen sense of smell. They will freeze in a certain position, or point, toward birds. After a bird has been shot, a retrieving dog will collect the game and return it to the hunter.

Bow Hunting

Some hunters like to use bows and arrows to bag their game. They find this type of hunting peaceful and relaxing. A bow and arrow are used to hunt big and small game. Most states grant bow hunters a longer hunting season than hunters who use guns. Although bow hunting is popular, it takes patience and practice to use this weapon.

The three basic types of bows are compound bows, recurve bows, and longbows. The most common bow used for hunting is the compound bow. An arrow will usually not travel as far as a bullet, so a hunter using a bow must quietly approach the prey to get close enough to hit it.

This hunter is using a compound bow. Compound bows were first made in the United States in the 1960s.

Early Hunters

People have hunted throughout history. The first hunters were **prehistoric** people. Scientists have found drawings that are over 20,000 years old of bison, wild horses, and cows on cave walls. Prehistoric people hunted these animals for food and clothing. These early hunters had to hunt to stay alive.

Over the years people have used many unusual hunting methods. For hundreds of years, cheetahs

Cheetahs are fast and powerful hunters. They can run as fast as 70 miles per hour (113 km/h).

The Native Americans of the Great Plains used bows and arrows to hunt bison.

were trained for hunting. Italians used cheetahs to hunt in the fifth century. In the eleventh and twelfth centuries, Russian princes also kept cheetahs for hunting. Akbar, a famous ruler in India, owned about 9,000 cheetahs during his reign in the sixteenth century.

Nature and Hunting

Many hunters are **conservationists**. They love nature and animals. Animals face many difficulties in nature, such as rough weather, **predators**, and sickness. Only the strongest stay alive. Each animal has a place in the food chain. If too many animals of one kind live in one area, this can upset the food chain.

Special groups in each state keep track of game animal populations. The hunting season for each animal is carefully decided based on the number of animals in the area. An animal may be hunted only during its hunting season. Hunters are allowed to take only a certain number of each kind of animal. In this way hunters help balance animal populations.

The season for hunting pheasant varies from state to state, but it usually falls between October and January.

Let's Go Hunting!

Hunting is a great way to learn about animals and spend time with a special adult. Hunting can teach you to carefully observe your surroundings, too. When you begin hunting, pay attention to landmarks, such as large trees or rocks, so you will remember your route. Remember to carry a map and compass to keep from getting lost.

While walking, look at the ground for animal tracks you can identify. Watch the leaves on a tree to establish the wind direction. Then you can approach an animal without your scent arriving first and scaring it away. Listen carefully. You may hear an animal rustling in a bush or a duck calling in the distance.

Look and listen all around you. Let's go hunting!

The ability to identify animal tracks is a useful skill for a hunter. *Inset:* A bear made this paw print.

Safety Tips

- Every state offers some type of hunter safety program. You should take the program your state provides before going out on your first hunt.

- Be sure to spend plenty of time practicing at a shooting range before you go hunting. This practice will allow you to become familiar with your weapon.

- Wear bright orange clothing while hunting so other hunters will recognize you.

- Always assume every gun is loaded, and handle it with care.

- While carrying any type of weapon, do not point it at anything other than your target.

- Shoot only at a target you can clearly see and recognize.

- When carrying a gun, keep the safety on at all times.

- Wear earplugs when you fire a gun.

- Don't leave a gun leaning on a tree or fence. It could fall and fire by itself.

- Know where the other hunters in your area are located at all times.

- Do not hunt with someone who is not following basic hunting safety rules.

Glossary

barrel (BAR-ul) The long part of a gun where the bullet or buckshot comes out.

blinds (BLYNDZ) Places where people hide to watch or shoot animals.

camouflage (KA-muh-flaj) A color or a pattern that matches the surroundings and helps hide something.

conservationists (kon-ser-VAY-shun-ists) People who want to protect nature.

elk (ELK) A very large kind of deer.

game (GAYM) Wild animals that are hunted for food.

pheasant (FEH-znt) Large, colorful birds that live on the ground.

predators (PREH-duh-terz) Animals that kill other animals for food.

prehistoric (pree-his-TOR-ik) Having to do with the time before written history.

quail (KWAYL) Small, stout birds that live on the ground.

scat (SKAT) Animal droppings.

scope (SKOHP) A metal tube with lenses inside that a hunter looks through to make something look larger.

targets (TAR-gits) Things that are aimed at.

waterfowl (WAH-ter-fowl) Water birds.

Index

Web Sites

Due to the changing nature of Internet links, PowerKids Press has developed an online list of Web sites related to this book. This site is updated regularly. Please use this link to access the list: www.powerkidslinks.com/adout/hunting/